ISBN: 9798327428317

Is it not a golden life that, upon one's death, the world around them feels a tragedy.

CONTENTS

LESSON ONE
LESSON TWO
LESSON THREE
LESSON FOUR
LESSON FIVE
LESSON SIX
LESSON SEVEN
LESSON EIGHT

Dedicated to my wonderful Mom,
the most resilient, wise, loving and
powerful woman I will ever know, and
the best kitchen dancer in the world.

Dedicated to my wonderful Dad, who
with amazing endurance, strength and
love, champions forward for us all.

Saying goodbye to your mother is impossible. Yet, shockingly, the final days with your mother can, somehow and remarkably, be the greatest days of your life, as final lessons in dignity, power, faith, love, and grace create golden, resonating and transformative memories.

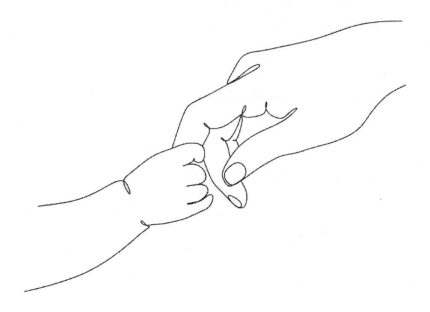

This is the story of the final life lessons taught by one mother, to one daughter, as the experience of death approached.

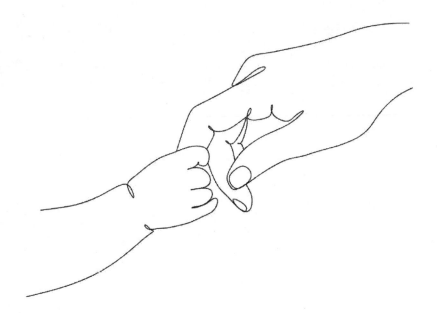

LESSON ONE: DANCE INTO THE STORM

This is the story of a mother and a daughter.

I am the *daughter*.

When I was a little girl, my mother and I would dance in our kitchen. Our dances were a part of my childhood, usually on Saturday mornings or lazy Sundays, sometimes a weeknight when she wasn't too tired – as my mother had a vibrant career, and somehow, she navigated all the time demands that come with having the strength to raise both a career and a family, all while discovering oneself in the process.

Our dances were not fancy, but they were fun.

Holding hands, twirling around, the older I got, the more ridiculous our moves grew, until we mostly just swayed and swirled about, silly chuckles in the air of the kitchen, our ridiculous dance moves in full view of the large window above our kitchen sink – putting us on display for our backyard neighbors to enjoy our frolicking for free.

Life is sometimes nothing more than random moments of twirling in the kitchen with your mother.

Those random moments most people do not remember with any scrutiny or sense of purposeful or mindful commitment to one's life journey – just a million random moments of silly smirks, twirls and clumsy paces by the light of the open refrigerator.

I don't know when it came … the last day I danced with my mother in the kitchen.

Obviously, there was a time, a day, that was our final kitchen dance. It could have been a random Saturday night when I was visiting, or maybe it was a few quick steps together when one of my kids were toddlers – I don't remember, and, though I can no longer ask her directly, I doubt highly my mother knew when our kitchen recital took its final bow.

My mother died a few months ago. She died the month of her birth, with me resting on her chest and holding my face to her own, as she drifted and drifted away.

Her death was difficult – for her, more than anyone, of course, and for the rest of us, it was an *unfathomable* experience.

Her death wasn't sudden, and yet, at the same time, was filled with urgency and an almost manic vibration of anticipation – the feeling you get when you might miss your plane, or you are getting ready to board a train, and realize you left your mobile phone in the car. My mother's death was not a peaceful flight to the hereafter, it was a deliberate, planned and organized task we undertook over a few random days in the chill of a changing season.

There was beauty. There was laughter. There was magic. There was love. But, in all that there was, in all that my mother's final days were, there existed also the vibration of

10

pensiveness – the unrest of the looming and, for me, the recognition of my beautiful mother's fading intent to live, and acceptance of the willingness to die.

My mother was ready to, as the hospice team members shared with us in loving and comfortable tones, die with dignity.

My mother wanted to die … with dignity.

This was very fitting for my mother, as she lived her life in all things dignified – the way she carried herself through life's storms, the way she served as the foundation of strength and support for our family, the way she embraced the devotion of her commitment to my father and our family as our heroine, our matriarch … our gold.

My mother may very well have been the most dignified woman of anyone I know. She was incredibly intuitive, overflowing with common sense, a lifelong learner, a secret explorer and, above all else, one who others could rely upon – one who others could love, and know they were loved even more greatly by her, in return.

My mother wanted to die … with dignity.

At the age of 75, she was exhausted with all that her physical ailments drained her of for the final years of her life, which unfortunately included multiple strokes and rapid kidney failure. After more hospital stays than one could hope to squeeze into 24 months, after multiple weeks spent in rehabilitation facilities, and following the reality of dialysis treatments – my mother, and her body, were done.

My mother wanted to die … with dignity.

11

She was ready to dance into the storm, like so many other storms she danced bravely into during her lifetime. With no fear, only a sense of acceptance, resolve and even wonder, she was ready to dance … to whatever was beyond.

I was ready to support her in this intention. I was not ready; however, to be the last of us remaining in this world, alone on the dance floor of life, wondering where my kitchen dance partner had gone without me.

I was ready to support her intention to dance into the unknown, as her body failed her, but I was not ready to be on the other side of her exit – leaving me to dance alone.

Remarkably, and unsurprisingly, my mother knew I felt I was not ready to let her dance away. She also knew, and expressed to me in loving terms, that I was, indeed, capable and ready for this unavoidable separation – that I could dance through the storm, with her, and dance through the joys and storms of a life to be lived without her.

My mother was an incredibly smart woman.

In our final days together, which is what this story is all about, those final few days of life together, those final few moments to celebrate our dance, my mother continued to be the devoted guide and instructor to me she had been my entire life.

In the quiet of our hours together, in the middle of the night, when the world was sleeping, I was gifted with the reinforcement of a *lifetime* of invaluable lessons my mother imparted to me, with the dignity of her actions, and the remarkable endurance she always possessed. She also taught me new lessons – lessons in how to be fearless in the face of powerful transformation, how to remain composed and inquisitive in the hours leading to one's final dance, and, above all else, how to remain true to one's own convictions and intentions – how to dance, with dignity, into the storm, and retain at all times the faith that, beyond the storm, the sun will rise.

My mother wanted to die ... with dignity.

Death, of course, is a transformation.

Transformations, of course, await us each of us, bringing with them pivotal turning points in our lives – moments that bring true love, bitter acceptance, great challenge, overwhelming drive, personal freedom and even, for the most *fortunate* of us, the opportunity to appreciate the memories of a random kitchen dance.

In my mother's final days, her transformation glowed with lessons for me to realize, absorb, and ultimately, share. None were less impactful than the strength and resolve it takes one, in life, and in death, the dance, bravely and with an open heart, and a mind of discovery, into any storm.

LESSON ONE: Dance into the storms of your life, with the strength and conviction that you have the fortitude to experience the storm, and the sunlight on the other side.

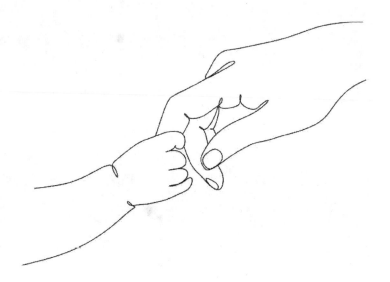

14

LESSON TWO:
IF YOU CANNOT MOVE …
DRIFT

There are so many days in our lives we do not anticipate experiencing. Subconsciously, of course, there is an undercurrent of acceptance, if not recognition, that these very days will eventually emerge out of the darkness – for us to experience and endure.

The death of your mother is one.

My mother was only 36 when she lost her own mother. Of course, her mother suffered debilitating health issues at a young age, so, in many ways, my mother lost the *opportunity* to have a sustained adult relationship with her mother when my mother was only the age of 20.

You see, when my mother was only a few months into her twentieth year, her own beautiful mother suffered a catastrophic stroke, which left her unable to be physically viable as the caring, devoted, and active mother she had always been to my mother, and my mother's three older siblings, not to mention the abundance of beautiful grandchildren already thriving in this world.

As it was, at the age of 20, barely an adult, and pregnant with her first child – *me* – my mother found herself readying to become a first-time mother, while reconciling the severity and permanence of her own mother's frailty.

Fortunately, my mother and father, young and in love, leaned on one another to make the best of difficult situations – lifelong lovers, lifelong partners, and, even more substantially, truly and deeply devoted lifelong friends.

For my mother, the loss of her own mother hit early.

I was fortunate. I was gifted with my mother until the age of 55. Two nights before my mother died, when we had already begun our steps forward with hospice care, we had hours of wonderful conversation, loaded with laughter and memories.

My mother was an exceptional storyteller!

I am going to say that *again*, because she deserves the emphasis on this accolade. You see, as it was, my father was a champion storyteller in his own right, incredibly entertaining, way too charismatic, boldly energized and, just funny – so much so that my mother often would enjoy his stories more than share her own in family groups and lively conversations. She loved his stories. Everyone did.

Still … my mother was an exceptional storyteller!

In our final shares together, as we talked for hours and hours, knowing our evenings of being able to do so were now dwindling fast, my mother shared some of my favorite stories of her youth – favorites, indeed! She talked about the time a neighbor on her street was convinced he saw a UFO, and the time she, as a little girl, spent hours and hours riding her bike miles and miles from her home on an adventure so many towns over that it was miraculous she got home in time for dinner. She told me of the wonderful pies and cakes her mother would bake for her, and the delicious dinners she always came home to after a day of exploring her world.

She also told me one of my favorite stories of a week spent in Atlantic City when she was a young teen. She and her friend, Gerry, were enjoying Atlantic City, with my mother's mother as their wonderfully watchful guardian. Of course, the teen girls still managed to almost drown in the Atlantic Ocean, despite the cautions of my trusting grandmother.

You see, the story, as my mother would tell it, has my mother and her friend playfully swimming in the rolling waves just a few steps into the Atlantic Ocean off the hot sands of Atlantic City. Swimming, swimming, paddling their feet and laughing, the girls swam, swam and swam, pushing their young bodies into the ocean ahead of them – fearless and free.

Until they realized … they had pushed out a bit further than they had intended. Out beyond the point where the waves begin to roll into peaks that then crash onto the dampened sands of the beach, the girls looked at one another – with worry in their eyes. Neither was an exceptional swimming, and both realized they could not touch the bottom – they were to far out, paddling on waves that were carrying them.

"We were out too far, we could have easily drowned if we began to panic," my mother told me, her voice just a whisper, but the story still resonating with power. "So, we just looked at each other, and pushed our shoulders forward, kicked our feet, and begin to just drift and drift and drift on the waves back to the beach. Boy, were we relieved to feel the sand under our feet again!"

My mother was always very good at calmy drifting forward. Despite the disappointments, burdens and trials of life, she always found it within her to remain calm under pressure, to stay focused on a goal of positivity, and to, above all else, lean toward improving circumstances, even if she had to drift.

You see, drifting is still moving.

Drifting is still believing in changing circumstances.

Drifting is still a decision – and, at times, the only one.

As my mother, herself, began to drift in her final days and hours and minutes toward a beach without a name, toward shored yet unexplored, to a place I could not drift with her, in that moment, she inspired me to accept what I would have to do once she was fully and completely gone.

I would have to drift.

Without her, I would feel perhaps lost, motionless in the waves of life, not quite able to reach my toes to feel the bottom, weightless in a cool sea of uncertainty, riding a tide unknown, to a place not yet discovered. Still, in my mother's stories, and in the examples, she gave as a woman of fortitude and strength in how she lived her own life, it was a gift to hear again, in her final storytelling moments with me, the strength one can find in drifting. After all, we can all find the strength to drift.

LESSON TWO: *If you cannot move, drift. Allow yourself to find your way forward, allow yourself to be carried in the right direction for your betterment – drift until you can swim, drift until you can walk, drift until you can feel.*

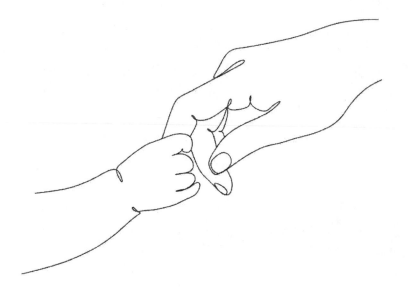

LESSON THREE:
WATCH THE MOVIE
MOONSTRUCK – ONCE A YEAR

My mother had a few favorite movies. She had excellent and diverse taste in entertainment. She loved stories of Scottish history, adventures and thrillers. She enjoyed police dramas, insightful documentaries, stories about real people, in real life, living for real. She enjoyed movies, television and books from the seemingly mundane to the spectacular, with themes of political, musical, historical and other directions.

Still … of all the entertainment she explored in her over seven decades, only one movie made it to the heights of recommendation – recommendation to be watched at least once a year. Two days before she died, we watched it.

The movie? Moonstruck.

What is Moonstruck? Well, for those of you who may not know, Moonstruck is an American romantic comedy from the 1980s starring the legendary Cher as *Loretta Castorini* , a widowed Italian American woman who falls in love with the passionate, quirky and somewhat estranged and generally angered younger brother of the Italian American gentleman she is engaged to wed. The names in the movie alone beg for attention: *Cosmo, Rose, Ronny, Johnny.* Nicholas Cage stars as *Ronny Cammareri*, and the movie boasts superstar power the likes of Olympia Dukakis, Vincent Gardenia, Danny Aiello and more. The movie, set in Brooklyn Heights, won numerous awards – and became a lifelong favorite of my mother. The way Cher's *Lorretta* stuns with her glow up, as she falls for Cage's wild *Ronny*.

Sure, my mother was a fan of Cher, but that was not the reason Moonstruck touched her heart for decades.

In Moonstruck, my mother, of Irish and English ancestry, saw glimmers of the Italian American family she married into, when my mother, a shy and stunning young lady from a remote Pennsylvania town, fell in love with a handsome, boisterous young man from the Italian American streets of South Philadelphia.

Moonstruck *somehow* encapsulated the charms of the Italian American family experience, while, at the same time, encouraged people to believe in the magical powers of true love, the passions that give us all life, the thickness of the generational ties the connect us all, and the mysterious and marvelous beauty and timeless experience of looking up at a glowing full moon – and, just perhaps, in the glancing, experience a sparkle of magic.

Moonstruck was a story that resonated with my mother's heart – as it did the hearts of millions – for its story of love, loss, more love, and the eternal power of family ties.

"Everyone should watch Moonstruck at least once every year," my mother told me, as we sat, holding hands, in the quiet of the room that would act as her last physical haven in this state of existence. "Moonstruck is such a good movie, I always cry when I watch it – I *always* cry."

Her tears, my mother told me, were for the love of the story, a romantic comedy layered in the reliability of family connections, the wonder of second chances, the thrill of discovering new passions and the charm of enjoying the simple things in life – like a bowl of spaghetti and meatballs. Her tears, my mother shared with me, were for the love story within Moonstruck – and the yearning of Loretta and Johnny, as they fell in love and, in the falling, pushed out of their respective despairs and darkness, learning, together, to embrace the simple, and glorious, moments of life under the moonlit sky above.

Moonstruck was, to my mother, a metaphor for life. A reminder to enjoy the people in your life, as you grow to discover possibilities and opportunities that may exist for you, under the watchful gaze of the moon.

"Moonstruck is such a great story," my mother told me, in her voice, barely a whisper. "It always makes me happy."

As my mother neared her final hours, we no longer watched movies. Instead, she slipped from real to remembrance, the moonlit charms of Moonstruck somehow transitioning to a metaphor of a slightly different nature for me – a story of love, family devotion, and hope.

LESSON THREE: *Watching a movie, or listening to a special song, or looking through a photo album – digital or in print – can transport you to a time of hope and remembrance, of dreams and desires, and, along with that, connect you through space and time to the emotions and sentiments felt deeply by those you loved most in life.*

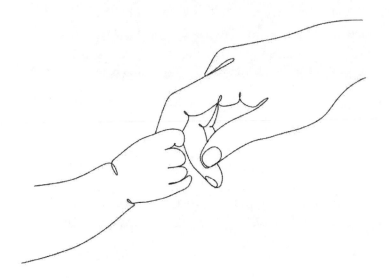

LESSON FOUR: KNOW YOUR LIMITS

 There is no such thing as a perfect person. How could there be? We are all flawed. We do (most of us anyway) the best we can, with the tools and intellect and experience life granted to us. There is no such thing as perfection, when it comes to any one person – in any one circumstance.

My mother; however, was a perfect person.

I realize that sounds like a contradiction. In fact, it is a glaring contradiction – and of course, my mother would be the first person to say, it is not true. Still, in all the ways that could arguably make a person *perfect*, or as close to perfection as one might become, my mother was, indeed, perfect.

She was the rock on which our family stood strong.

She was the grace on which our family rested.

When I was a little girl, my mother and I would take walks around a lovely little lake near our home. Our walks would some days be long, and some days short, depending on how much time we each had – and how in the mood we were, respectively. As I grew older, into my teens, we would walk separately. Me, going a little faster, making more laps around the lake, listening to my favorite music of the

25

moment as I outpaced my Mom, who strolled at a more reasonable pace, taking in the beauty of nature surrounding the lake, and stopping from time to time to chat with other walkers, and those just resting on benches around the lake's treelined pathways.

I walked at my pace.

My mother walked at her pace.

When we were ready to go, we joined back up, and got in the car, and headed back to the house together. In my mother's final days, we walked about those walks. We talked about the little lake, and what peaceful times we had just walking together around it.

We talked about how we would sometimes get ice cream afterwards, and how sometimes when we got back to the house, we would make popcorn. We talked about the world when I was little, and how much she loved being my mother – and mother to my younger brother.

We talked about holidays and birthdays and rainy days and lots and lots of days in which we walked together – and separately.

"You know," my mother told me, sipping water from a thin straw in her room on her final day of consciousness. "I am not afraid to die, I am just sorry for all that I am going to miss – all that I won't see, because I won't be here."

What do you say to your mother when she says those words to you? How do you find the positivity in a moment like that – when all you want to do is break into pieces?

Fortunately, I was raised by a very strong woman.

"Well," I told my mother. "Don't think of that, everything is going to be alright, we all love you, you know the directions of so many of us, you set us all on good paths, and, before you know it, we'll be walking together again – just like that, just in a blink, we'll all be together again, you're just a little bit ahead."

My mother smiled softly, little tears rolling over her face that looked, somehow, serenely joyful, and utterly calm.

I think in that moment I realized...

She was outpacing me at this time.

Walking on the steps of her journey to the hereafter, it was my mother pushing her pace forward, picking up momentum, as I slacked back a bit, on the path we were on together – she was pacing ahead of me, walking beyond the limits of which I could keep up.

She was on a journey, with limits only she could define.

I was on a journey, reliant upon her limits.

Yet, together, we were a mother, and a daughter, walking around a lake, on our own terms, within our own limits, knowing that, at the end of our respective strides, even though we would walk around the lake at our own paces, we would, at our respective walks' conclusions, meet and, together, go home.

LESSON FOUR: In life, sometimes, we walk side by side with the people who matter most to us. Sometimes, though, we may walk separately – due to differences in opinions, or changes beyond our control, or just the general moods of the day. Ultimately, the hope and blessed reality may very well be that after every step we take, together or separately, we arrive at the same place of glory, if only in our ability to believe.

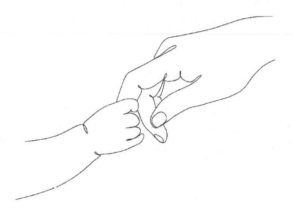

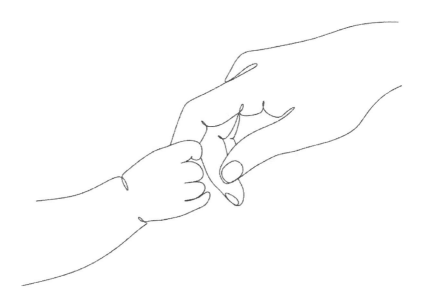

LESSON FIVE:
CLOSE YOUR EYES & BREATHE

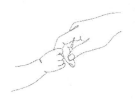

The day before my mother died, she told me the story of the bee – a story I heard many times, but always enjoyed.

Here is her story:

When my mother was a little girl, maybe no more than six or seven, she was very much a tomboy – spending hours each day, especially in summers, outside on adventures she navigated either alone or, more often, with neighborhood kids out for the same adventurous times.

My mother never took for granted the freedom and fun of her childhood, one spent with bruised knees from near misses, with dirty hands and feet from real play, all day, in very real dirt.

One afternoon, she was sitting in the sun in the grass of her own backyard. Unattended, as children were at a time when it was normal to let your kid out for the day, she stretched her little body over the warm, dewy grass on a summer afternoon painted just for her.

As she sat up, leaning her little body back against her hands which were anchored to the dirt, her bare knees shifted up and bent toward the warm sunrays. Too perfect a moment, a bee landed on one of her exposed little bent knees. It was a very, very big bee.

30

Alone in her backyard, with just the grass and the sky watching her, she looked at the bee, which sat on her knee with no other place to go.

My mother was afraid.

What did she do?

"I closed my eyes," my mother told me, her voice gently flowing from her tired body.

Sure enough, the little girl who would one day be my mother closed her eyes, and quietly breathed, and breathed and breathed softly some more. When she gathered up the courage to open her eyes, the bee was gone. Only her bare knee, glistening in the summer sun, was in her youthful gaze. No longer afraid, and feeling grateful, she continued to enjoy her summer afternoon, alone in her yard, with the sun, the grass and, somewhere, her new friend, buzzing off on its next adventure.

There is a calculated randomness to the stories we hear in our lifetimes.

Sometimes, we hear them when we are afraid, other times when we are overjoyed – and sometimes when we are trying to find the courage to be the people we aspire to be.

LESSON FIVE: In her retelling of this favorite story from my childhood, or rather, her childhood, my mother's gentle lesson to breathe through moments of fear can help one find courage in the unknown, and bravery in a patience aligned with hope. Fear not the bee, fear not what frightens you – close your eyes, breath, and experience the moment.

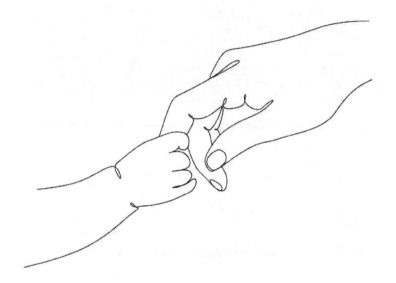

LESSON SIX:
REALITY WILL DICTATE

In the weeks leading up to my mother's final hospitalization, we had just begun dialysis treatments.

Her kidneys were failing – rather, they had failed almost entirely. Her bladder was barely functional as well, and an infection overcame her entire body, making all the failures of her physical frame even more difficult to navigate. Her blood pressure could not be controlled. Complications to her dialysis treatments surfaced. She experienced a few small strokes, endured with persistent infection and complications too numerous to mention. There were several rapid response calls to her hospital room in the weeks leading to her departure from this earth, with teams of nurses and doctors working to stabilize her.

She even got COVID.

Exhausted and quite frankly *'over everything'* she began to resolve herself, and the rest of us, of her trajectory.

At some point, during her final hospitalization, she decided her life would end soon, if for no other reason that she could feel, despite all hopes and medical best efforts, despite our wishes, her body could no longer keep up the fight.

Why did my mother always have to be right?

Sure enough, as her days in hospital care turned into her final days in hospice in a rehabilitation facility set amongst tall trees, the tone shifted from *'what more can be done'* to *'what shall we talk about'* with the rapid pace of panic and chaos replaced by an uncomfortable acceptance, a more relaxed, if not forced sense of calm, in recognizing the inevitable circumstances we found ourselves existing.

Reality will dictate.

This was a saying my mother would use many times in my life, sharing this sentiment with my brother, with me, and anyone who needed to hear some stoic words of wisdom and resolution.

My mother was a pragmatist.

She was a dreamer, too.

She was a woman sprinkled with hope and wishes, wrapped up in a package of pure common sense and appropriate cynicism. She was smarter than most people, and wiser than her years – even when younger.

Now, faced with a new reality, perhaps her greatest reality, and one that we were facing together, with her, as best as we could as a family devastated by impending loss, we somehow, thanks to her calming disposition, embraced the reality of the moment.

My amazing father, my brother, and our dear friends and family who were a part of my mother's final days in her human form, all of us were facing a reality that was being dictated – part by the tides of life, and part by my mother, herself.

My mother did not fear reality.

She taught us to face reality – and face it with strength.

While she made it look so easy, in her final days and hours, she surpassed even her own lifelong demonstrations of the courageous, resilient and pragmatic person that was her. She was ready for her reality, facing it with a resolve reserved for kings and queens, saints and prophets.

As I held her hands, rested my head on her chest, and hugged her in her moments of wake and sleep, of drifting off into somewhere else just before the drift became her final journey, I realized her lifelong lesson of ***reality will dictate*** was a true mantra of maturity and strength.

There are times in life, times that call us to be stronger than we hope we will ever need to be – times of reality.

Brutal, cold and unwavering. Still, in these times of reality, these shocking and shaking moments beyond our ability to shift or avoid, we find our greatest pieces of ourselves.

Reality, as my mother would tell me, will dictate … for us all. How we decide to face the dictation remains with *each* of us. For my mother, she faced her final reality – her impending death – with a bravery unmatched, and a fearless sparkle of royalty.

35

She was neither afraid, nor in denial, of the reality being dictated to her. She feared it not, denied it not, and in facing her reality with a dignity only she could command, she inspired us all.

LESSON SIX: Life is hard. There are often moments that call us to live in a reality that breaks our hearts, one in which we must purely function, as we drift forward in life. Nonetheless, reality will dictate – and it is the wisest of us, who will stand strong and brave in the face of the dictation.

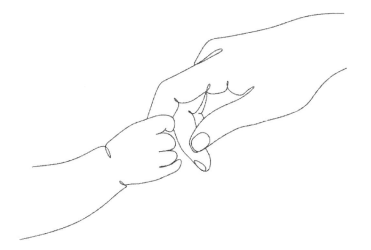

LESSON SEVEN: KNOW WHO YOU ARE

 Once my mother began the hospice journey forward to her next adventures, beyond this lifetime, her days were rapid and short. It was only two days – two days off certain medications and procedures, two days removed from the pains of dialysis, two days closer to her reunion with her own mother.

Two final days for me, with my mother.

At first, our plan – and hope – was to bring her home. I wanted her to be in her own room, surrounded by her own things, with me by her side, with my father and brother and family and friends – all assembled in the home she made for each of us to enjoy.

Unfortunately, her condition was too unstable – she was too delicate, too fragile to move from the rehabilitation facility that welcomed her after her final hospitalization. I had failed her – I could not bring her home. I could not transport her without her feeling great pain, regardless of the medical transport service. I could not navigate her end-of-life care in a way that would prohibit unnecessary discomfort. Plus, she was too unstable, medically, to move.

I could not get her home.

38

In one of our many final moments together, holding hands, I looked at my mother and, through tears, told her our situation.

"Mom, after a lifetime of taking on more than I could do, after a lifetime, so far, of taking on more than I could manage, I am so sorry, but this is too much for me to manage. I don't know if you can endure the transport. I don't know, if we can do this – if we can get you home," I cried to my mother, holding her hands as she held mine, both of us clutching one another, in a moment of graceful comfort, and, for me, traumatic sorrow, and even shame.

My mother was serene.

She put her hands on my face, and looking into my eyes she removed all of my guilt and disappointment.

"I *know*," she told me. "It's alright, I am fine and comfortable right here. This room has a very good feeling, don't you think?"

My mother had always tried to encourage me, throughout my lifetime, to manage my time, my commitments and my responsibilities in more tempered ways.

Unlike my mother, I always had difficulties regulating myself – taking on too much, overextending my commitments, rushing to meet demands only I placed on myself. Trying to make big things happen, when the bigness was too great to be managed.

If only I knew myself better.

My mother knew me very, very well.

In the patience of her final days and hours with me, a sacred window of time in which she and I operated outside the parameters of normal life, she continued to show me the way to embrace what I could reasonably do – and accept my strengths, and limitations.

As we resigned ourselves to stay safely and securely where we were, as we resigned ourselves that, indeed, we would not be going home together, we drifted our conversation to recipes, discussing everything from our family's cornbread recipe, to how to make a Thanksgiving turkey – and more.

We talked about our favorite holiday recipes, and the ways to prepare some of my father's favorite dishes. In those moments, in our laughter and joy in talking about uplifting topics, from recipes and holiday memories, the quaint room in which my mother would drift toward death felt cozy and comfortable – soothing and warm, almost like home.

LESSON SEVEN: In life, many times, one may try to be bigger and stronger than is possible in a given moment in time. One may strive to take on more than is reasonable, even make promises one cannot keep – despite hopes. In these moments, as my mother taught me in her loving and patient ways, the important thing is to be the best version of yourself in the moment in which you are existing – to know who you are, where you are, and that, no matter where you may go in life, you always carry home within you.

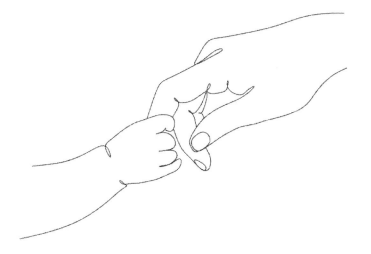

LESSON EIGHT:
LOVE MORE, AND *MORE*

The night before my mother died, we were watching television. It was very late in the evening, and we were very wide awake – at least, I was.

My mother was growing weaker, and it was becoming more difficult for her to talk to me, to stay on the same level of existence with me.

As we took a break from our tears and laughter, often mixed together for reasons neither of us could sustain, I told my mother how much I loved her.

Her response to me was … *I love you more.*

My mother loved me more.

My mother … loved me more.

How lucky are so many of us truly fortunate people in life, to have mothers who love us more. I always knew my mother was a mother beyond devotion, dedicated to our family, to the betterment of all who would cross her path.

When my mother told me she loved me more, I thought to myself, how blessed I have been in this life, to have had a mother who loved me as much as my mother.

I have two daughters.

I love them more, too.

42

And it is because I had such a loving mother that I, myself, am guilty of the same reward, to love my children, more than I love myself, and, in that love, in that confession of absolute devotion, lives an eternity of enduring support and comfort. My mother loved me more – and even in her dying hours, she, with grace, put my needs as her daughter, before her own needs as a woman at the end of life.

My mother loved me … more.

In her final moments, when she could no longer speak her love to me, or my brother, or my father, or her sisters, or our family and friends, in her final moments we could feel how much she loved each of us, for all we were, and all we were still to be, with her forever with us, in new and enduring ways. My mother loved more … and because she did, her love remains in every moment we drift forward with her very much alive in our hearts for all eternity.

LESSON EIGHT: Life is short. Love more. Embrace the people who have made your life one of joy. Embrace the people who have shared your sorrows, hopes, excitements, dreams, prayers, glories, downfalls and triumphs. Give all your heart to the people who have made your soul sing. Be a force of positivity and strength, to those who need you more. Be the one to love more … and love even more.

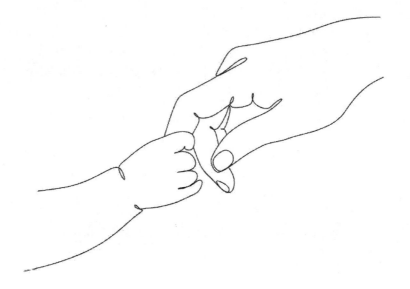

Made in the USA
Columbia, SC
09 December 2024

48779458R00026